George Melville Baker

Messmates

A drama in three acts

George Melville Baker

Messmates
A drama in three acts

ISBN/EAN: 9783337343804

Printed in Europe, USA, Canada, Australia, Japan

Cover: Foto ©Andreas Hilbeck / pixelio.de

More available books at **www.hansebooks.com**

MESSMATES

A Drama in Three Acts

BY

GEORGE M. BAKER

CHARACTERS.

ALVAH MORGAN, a speculator.
RICHARD CARTER, owner of the "Seabright."
NAT. TAYLOR, captain of the "Seabright."
TEDDY MORGAN, a runaway.
WOLF, a stowaway.
CRUMBS, the steward.
GRACE MORGAN, Alvah's daughter.
POLLY TAYLOR, the captain's pet.
ARABELLA CARAWAY, Alvah's sister.
PHILLIS, Grace's maid.

COSTUMES.

———————

Alvak. Age fifty. Gray crop wig, short side whiskers, blue yachting suit, — except on last entrance in second act, when he should appear in trousers and shirt only, collar loose, the appearance of having hastily arisen from bed.

Captain. Age fifty. Bald gray wig, full beard running from ear to ear around the throat, chin and lip bare, face ruddy and good-natured; blue yachting coat with brass buttons; cap, blue trousers, blue shirt. In first act no kerchief, in others black kerchief and waistcoat.

Richard. Red hair, mustache and chin-beard, eye-glasses; blue yachting suit, rather natty in appearance; rapid in speech and gesture, but very cool.

Teddy. Act I. Curly hair, sailor shirt with blue collar, white sailor trousers, black kerchief, naval cap with " Seabright " in gilt letters on the front. Acts II. and III. Change to blue shirt and trousers.

Wolf. Act I. Blue trousers, white sailor shirt with torn sleeve showing bare right arm; leathern belt; red handkerchief or red cap on head. Acts II. and III. Blue sailor trousers and shirt, black neckerchief, gray wig, mustache and side whiskers all one piece, chin smooth.

Crumbs. White trousers, jacket, and apron; white naval cap with " Seabright " in gilt letters; darky face and wig.

Grace. Act I. Pretty yachting suit. Act II. Dark dress, with white collar, cuffs, apron, and nurse's cap. Act III. Pretty summer suit, suitable for the tropical change of climate.

Polly. Yachting suit with dark straw hat, " Seabright " in gilt letters. In Act II., for first entrance, pea-jacket, and imitation in black glazed cloth of a " sou'wester " hat. Act III. Same as first.

Arabella. Act I. Rather plump figure, in summer costume, to suit age, about forty; not bad looking. In Act III. drop plumpness, but wear same costume. A slightly gray curly wig, parted on side, or corkscrew curls and red wig, at the pleasure of the performer.

COSTUMES.

Phillis. Bright mulatto girl, with the faintest tinge of color, gold hoop earrings, neat and tasty dress ; or, a coal-black negress, to suit the pleasure of the performer, — the author's preference being for the former. In the latter case, give the part the dialect used by " Crumbs."

NOTES.

Act I. Wolf makes his first appearance from a "transom." This is a long box, and may interfere with the central entrance, which should be wide. Instead, a trap-door in C. of stage will serve, and where it is practicable is much to be preferred, as a stowaway would be likely to secrete himself in the hold. Where both are in the way, or not convenient, use the L. U. E. Another method is to have a " locker " or cupboard L. of C.

Act II. Wolf and Teddy should have change of costume for the rescue, both to appear in trousers and shirt only. These should be duplicated, and the suit worn on their re-appearance should be "dripping " in appearance, a spangling of isinglass helping the illusion.

In this act, the "roaring of the gale," the "wind whistling through the rigging," and the motion of the vessel will all add interest to the storm-scene. The " roaring " and "whistling " are produced by placing a humming-top on the spindle of a spinning-wheel; slow and rapid revolutions will produce imitations of whistling and roaring in a wonderful manner. The "motion" may be made imaginary by the rolling and pitching of the characters.

MESSMATES.

A DRAMA IN THREE ACTS.

ACT I.—OUTWARD BOUND.

The action of the three acts is in the cabin of the yacht "Seabright."

SCENE.—C., *in flat, the companion-way, with two steps. From the upper step, entrances* R. *and* L. *Back of the steps a marine picture on the wall, brass hand-rails* R. *and* L. *of steps. Portières over companion-way;* L. *of companion-way, against flat, practicable transom covered with red. Two doors on* R., *two on* L., *leading to state-rooms, indicated as* R. 1 *and* R. 2, L. 1 *and* L. 2, *No.* 1 *nearest audience. Entrances* R *and* L., *first* E.; *swinging-lamps* R. *and* L. *on flat. Table* R., *back, covered with a white cloth, to show red cloth when removed. On table, breakfast dishes, a half-cut bone of ham, a plate of bread, easy chair* R. *of table;* L., *half way up stage, small table with chair beside it, red cover on table.* CRUMBS *discovered back of table* R., *picking up dishes and placing them on waiter.* PHILLIS *dusting at table* L. *Raise curtain with nautical music — "A Life on the Ocean Wave," or any familiar air.*

CRUMBS (*flourishing a pitcher*). O Miss Phillis, Miss Phillis! it's jes' what ole Parson Johnson said, "Dis am a hollow world." "Man cometh up like de sparrargrass, and he goeth out like de hoppergrass."

> "Life 'tis a strife, 'tis a bubble, 'tis a dream;
> And man he am a little boat a-floatin' down de stream."

And de fust ting he knows he strikes a snag, and dat leetle boat am upsot,—and de man, de man, oh, whar am he?"

PHILLIS. Why, don't you know, Mr. Crumbs? Jes' now

he's pickin' up dishes in the cabin of the "Seabright," and the snag that upset his little boat was jes' a little mite of a mitten.

CRUMBS. Oh! dis am a whale ob tears, a honeycomb ob bones.

PHILLIS. Honey! La, Mister Crumbs, you mean catacomb?

CRUMBS. O Sofy Sassafras! de idol of dis aching heart, de girl I lef behind me!

PHILLIS. What, Sophie! Is this the cause of all your groaning?

CRUMBS. Ob course. Wa'n't we to be married las' night? Wa'n't de isters cooked, and de ice-cream friz, and de parson dar, when de cap'n bust in like a cyclorama, and ordered me aboard in half an hour, case we were off in an hour? Didn't de meeting break up in disgust? didn't de bride tar her har? didn't ole Sassafras lif' his boot? and didn't de parson howl for his fee?

PHILLIS. And within two hours you, a man I had never seen before, told me I was the object of your adoration, and offered me your heart and hand.

CRUMBS. Dat's so. And you refused de balm ob consolation axed for, — refused de faithful heart.

PHILLIS. That's forgette'n the "girl he left behind," in an hour. Mr. Crumbs, I'm afraid your heart and your face are of the same complexion, very black, and neither will suit me.

CRUMBS. Well, you jes' wait until you find dar's no chowder for — for de secon' table, dat de fishballs an' de griddles am missin' when you get in to breakfas', dat dar's no graby for de roas' beef, dat de turkey hab taken to hisself wings and flowed away, den — den tink ob me. Ef I can't touch your heart any oder way, I'll try what poor fare will do.

PHILLIS. That would be mean.

CRUMBS. All's fair in lub.

PHILLIS. Oh, you don't frighten me! I've only to complain to my lady's father, Mr. Morgan.

CRUMBS (*comes down*). Dat ole man! Phillis, dar's somethin' wicked about him. I was in de cabin here las' night, ebery body turned in, when dat ole man come creepin' out ob his stateroom. Seemed to be walkin' in his sleep. He jes' stood an' wrung his hands and groaned, — how he did groan! (*Imitates as he speaks.*)

PHILLIS. Worse than you did when your little boat was upset?

CRUMBS. Don't fool. He jes' wrung his hands and groaned, and muttered, " I've murdered him! Why did he swim after the boat? How did he know I hab his gold? he swam — he swam — he swam, — and then he caught hold of de boat." De ole man was doin' it all, Phillis, swimmin' jes' so, and den he said, " I struck him wid de oar, and down he sunk, down, down, down; " an' den de ole man groaned some more, an' wrung his hands some more, an' crept off to his bunk. I tell you, Phillis, somethin' dreful gwine to happen, you'd better get somefin' to cling to when de trouble begins. You'd better take me afore I make any oder engagement.

PHILLIS. Yes, to the next girl you meet; think I'll try the poor fare first. You say you saw Mr. Morgan last night?

CRUMBS. Sartain sure.

PHILLIS. He must have been dreaming.

CRUMBS. He's got somethin' on his mind; I've got a fellow feelin' for him, I know what it is to suffer; an' if you had any feelin' for a fellow who's got a fellow feelin' for de ole man —

PHILLIS. Oh, don't bother! I'm not in the market for marrying. If I were, I should not be satisfied with Crumbs. (*Exit* L.)

CRUMBS (*goes back to table*). Nice girl dat Phillis; but proud and haughty. Nebber mind, when we get out to sea she'll be glad to hab somethin' to lean to, and den dis smitten bosom will be in demand. (*With waiter piled with dishes, exit* R. *first entrance.*) (*Music pianissimo. The cover of locker is lifted, and* WOLF *appears looking cautiously about.*)

WOLF (*stepping out*). Ah, the coast is clear, at last! Ten mortal hours I've been cramped in that locker (*stretches himself*). Oh, it's glorious to feel once more the free air, to stretch my aching limbs. (*Looks up companion-way.*) She's under way: I can hear the ripple of the water as her sharp bow cleaves the waves. A snug craft this. We're off, and the stowaway undiscovered. What is my next move? I cannot live in that box. (*Shivers.*) I need food : I'm as hungry as a wolf. (*Sees table.*) Ah, the lovesick steward has not quite cleared the table ; and, as I have a fellow feeling for unhappy lovers, I'll finish the job for him. (*Takes ham and bread from plate and platter.*) I hate to steal ; let hunger bear the theft,

I'll be its unwilling accomplice. (*Places food in locker.*) Off for Bermuda. It's a long trip for a yacht, but she's a beautiful sea-boat. Ah, visitors. Into your nest, you wolf. (*Gets into locker, and stands with hand on lid, listening.*)

(*Song outside.*)

" A wet sheet and a flowing sea,
  And a wind that follows fast,
And fills the wide and rustling sail,
  And bends the gallant mast,
And bends the gallant mast, my boys,
  Till like an eagle free,
Away our good ship flies, and leaves
  Columbia on our lea," etc.

(*During the song* TEDDY *appears in companion-way, polishing the hand-rails. Just as it concludes, he steps into cabin, and at the same moment* WOLF *sinks into locker, closing the lid.*)

TEDDY. So this is the cabin, the sacred retreat deckhands are forbidden to enter. (*Sits on locker.*) Jolly place, of course, since every thing about is of the same order. Oh, it's just gorgeous! no more study, no more recitations, but three weeks of solid fun on the jolly old wet ocean with those tarry chaps of the fo'castle, whose voices are never so musical as when on the high sea. I'm afraid my good old dad will hardly agree with me when he finds I have slipped my cable and left Harvard to mourn my loss. What's the odds? I've learned, in my short nautical experience, that "there's a sweet little cherub that sits up aloft to take care of the life of poor Jack;" so I'll trust to luck for the reconciliation which always comes to runaways who seek a life on the ocean wave, and the famous calf that is forever fattening for the prodigal's return. (*Sings.*)

" A wet sheet and a flowing sea."

(*Enter* CRUMBS, R. I E.)

CRUMBS. Avast dar. (TEDDY *rises.*) Do you take dis place for a conserbatory ob music? Ef de cap'n wants to get up a consort he *may* send for you. What you doin' into de cabin anyway?

TEDDY. I was sent to polish the hand-rails.

CRUMBS (*at table*). Polish hand-rails? well, I guess not. Whar's de ham? Whar's de bread? Ef you've done polishing dat ham-bone, I'll take it.

TEDDY. I've touched nothing.

CRUMBS. Won't do, sailor man, won't do. I don't keer if a man wants to make a hog of hisself filling up wid ham, but when he bones ham, common politeness should teach him to bring back de bone ob de ham he boned.

TEDDY. Shut up. Do you want to bring the whole ship's crew down here?

CRUMBS. Well, you jes bring back dat ham-bone, dat's all I ax ob you. (*Exit with platter and plate* R. I E.)

TEDDY. Our ebony steward seems to require a bit of polishing himself.

(*Song outside,* POLLY.)

" My Bonnie lies over the ocean,
My Bonnie lies over the sea ;
My Bonnie lies over the ocean,
Oh, bring back my Bonnie to me."

(*Appears in companion-way.*)

" Bring back, bring back, bring back my Bonnie to me, to me," etc.

TEDDY. The captain's jolly little daughter.

POLLY (*on stage*). Anybody stirring ?

TEDDY. No one but me : I'm at your service. Steward just now wanted me to bring back his bone. I couldn't do it, you know, but I might bring back your Bonnie for you if you'd tell me where to look for her.

POLLY. Ha, ha! Funny, ain't you? You're the green hand.

TEDDY. The green hand?

POLLY. Who shipped as an able seaman. The moment I clapped my weather-eye on you —

TEDDY. Beg pardon, which is your weather-eye?

POLLY. Ha, ha! an able seaman you! I don't believe you know the main hatch from the gaff topsail.

TEDDY. Oh, yes; I do. The gaff topsail is the what-you-may-call-it abaft the fore peak, and the main hatch, the main hatch —

POLLY. Well, the main hatch —

TEDDY. Is where they keep the chickens, of course.

POLLY. Ha, ha, ha! you an able seaman! You are an impostor.

TEDDY. And you the jolliest little sailor that ever climbed

the foretop bobstay, or spliced the main brace in short stays. How's that for nautics?

POLLY.   Worse and worse: you are an impostor.

TEDDY.   With tears in my eyes I confess it.

POLLY.   Then, why are you here?

TEDDY.   On a wager.

POLLY.   A wager?   Haven't I seen you at Cambridge?

TEDDY.   Shouldn't wonder; I was at Harvard.   We're always on exhibition.   Jolly place, Harvard.

POLLY.   I think I've noticed you passing my window.

TEDDY.   Have you, though?   Deuced kind of you to remember it.   The fellows would be green with envy if they knew it.

POLLY.   Well, the wager?

TEDDY.   I made a wager with Cy Goodwin.   Cy's a soph: I'm a fresh, you see.

POLLY.   I see.

TEDDY.   Well, I made a wager with Cy, that I'd get a formal introduction to you before he could; and yesterday I found out you were going on this cruise.   Cy found it out too; and, as he's a good yachtsman, he shipped for the cruise.   I couldn't let him get ahead of me in that way, so I shipped too.

POLLY.   For the purpose of getting an introduction to me.   That was cool.

TEDDY.   Coolness is the one state of the collegiate thermometer which the Harvard man diligently freezes to.

POLLY.   And how do you propose to win your wager?

TEDDY.   If you'll kindly name some friend of yours on board.

POLLY.   Oh, certainly; there's my father, the captain.

TEDDY.   Capital idea.   I'll ask him.

POLLY.   Do.   Only let me know when the trouble begins.

TEDDY.   Trouble?

POLLY.   Yes; for when a common sailor asks such a favor of his captain, he's likely to be strung up to the mainmast, keel-hauled, or set adrift in a jolly-boat.

TEDDY.   Which wouldn't be jolly at all.   We'll pass the captain.

POLLY.   Then there's Mr. Alvah Morgan.

TEDDY (*aside*).   Great Scott! my dad.

POLLY.   Miss Grace Morgan —

TEDDY (*aside*). My sister —

POLLY. Mrs. Arabella Caraway —

TEDDY. My aunt. — Do you mean to say those people are on board?

POLLY. They are. Do you know them?

TEDDY. Oh, no (*aside*)! I must disown the whole lot.

POLLY. You might ask them. By the way, what is your name?

TEDDY. Tom Tucker.

POLLY. I don't believe it.

TEDDY. Miss Taylor! on the word of a fresh —

POLLY. A fresh who is trying to pass himself off for an old salt. If you dare to ask anybody, I'll have you put in irons for the rest of the voyage. There is a wide difference between the cabin and the fo'castle, the captain's daughter and a common sailor. Keep your distance. (*Exit* C., *singing*.)

"Bring back, bring back, bring back my Bonnie to me, to me."

TEDDY. (*Watches her off. Enter* CRUMBS, *takes off the table-cloth while she is singing, then as her voice dies away in the distance sings, watching* TEDDY R. I E.)

"Bring back, bring back, bring back dat ham-bone to me, to me."

(TEDDY *shies his cap at him; exit* CRUMBS *repeating*.)

TEDDY (*picking up cap*). The situation is getting decidedly interesting; I've run away into the bosom of my family. They must have come on board after dark. Here's a pretty how d'ye do. Well, impudence, befriend me.

(*Enter* MRS. CARAWAY *from stateroom* I R.)

ARABELLA. My good man, have you seen a green — Good gracious! it's Teddy. Teddy Morgan, where did you drop from?

TEDDY (*in a gruff voice, hitching his trousers*). Shiver my timbers! bang my top-lights, and keel-haul me, marm. You've spoke the wrong ship.

ARABELLA. Good gracious, what a likeness!

TEDDY. Don't call me any landlubberly names; I'm Tom Tucker of the larboard watch ahoy, a rattlin' reefer, a double-decker, pickled in salt and soused in brine.

CAPTAIN (*outside*). Below there, Tom Tucker, ahoy! On deck, lively, lad, lively.

TEDDY. Ay, ay, sir! — My sarvice to you, marm, I'm piped

to quarters; and when duty calls, Tom Tucker is on deck, larboard, starboard, and amidships. (*Exit up companion-way, singing.*)

"A wet sheet and a flowing sea."

ARABELLA.   Can I believe my own eyes? our Ted's nose, the same mouth, that mischievous twinkle in his eyes.   Tom Tucker, indeed! as if I shouldn't know my own nephew!

(*Enter* GRACE *from stateroom* I L.)

GRACE.   Well, aunt, how comes on the unpacking?

ARABELLA.   O Grace, I've had such a turn!   There's a sea-monster on board this ship who's the image of our Teddy.

GRACE.   A   sea-monster!   not   very   complimentary   to Teddy.

ARABELLA.   I believe it's the boy himself; and he's a rattlin' reefer, and a double-decker, and he's going to shiver all the timbers in the ship.

GRACE.   Teddy is safe in college, aunt.

ARABELLA.   I'll believe it when I see him there.   Now you watch these sailors, especially one Tom Tucker, who's pickled in salt and soused in brine.   If he ain't Ted, I'm crazy.

GRACE.   Only a resemblance.   Aunt, Teddy is deep in his studies; I should as soon think of meeting Horace Gaylord here as brother Ted.   Where's father?

ARABELLA.   I heard him moving in his stateroom just now, and there, there's mine in such a mess.   It will take me a week to get to rights. (*Exit to stateroom* R. I.)

GRACE (*sits at table* L.).   This hasty departure, this sudden fancy for a trip to Bermuda; this yacht, the property of Richard Carter!   No farewell message to Horace Gaylord: what will he think of me?   I have long suspected that my father did not favor the man I love; but so kind and indulgent has he always been, I never looked for any strong opposition.

(*Enter* MORGAN *from stateroom* R. 2.)

MORGAN.   Ah, Grace! come on deck.   We are running swiftly out of port, and you have only time for a parting glance at the home we leave behind.

GRACE.   But why leave it?   Why are we going?

MORGAN.   For your health, my girl.   You have not been looking well of late; and when Richard Carter proposed this trip in his beautiful yacht, I eagerly seized the opportunity to benefit you.

GRACE. But why was I forbidden to communicate our departure to Horace Gaylord? Why this flitting in the night? Why this mystery?

MORGAN. It's more romantic.

GRACE (*rising*). 'Tis a cruel wrong to an honorable man who loves me, 'tis an attempt to favor the advances of another whom I can never accept.

MORGAN. Robert Carter is an honest man, who has acquired wealth —

GRACE. Ah, wealth! that is the loadstone that attracts worldly fathers. The happiness of their children is a secondary consideration.

MORGAN. You are bitter. Is it a crime to desire to see my daughter well settled in life?

GRACE. You are not a poor man; your wealth will abundantly portion both Teddy and me.

MORGAN. My wealth may vanish in a single day. Speculation, by which I win and lose, is a mocking devil who lures men to destruction over golden-paved roads, whose beds are honeycombed with pitfalls. If you are wise you will listen to Richard Carter, and let this struggling lover go.

GRACE. Richard Carter's millions do not tempt me; I have given my heart to the man who struggles, in whom I have faith, that, true as steel, he will cut his way through all obstacles, and win fame and fortune.

MORGAN. I will never give my consent.

GRACE. I think you will in time.

MORGAN. No, no! Far back in the record of my past life there is an entry I would gladly erase, one bitter experience that haunts my sleep. Something in his face recalls it. His voice makes me shudder, the touch of his hand chills me. We must put him out of our lives.

GRACE. Father!

MORGAN. You cannot understand this. 'Tis not necessary that you should. 'Tis my wish you should forget him.

GRACE. And you thought that separation would serve your purpose. Do not deceive yourself. I love him with all my heart. You are too good to make my life unhappy, too just to wrong him, so I will wait for your better nature to do him justice; if that fails, I have still my dear dead mother's advice to comfort me.

MORGAN.   What was that?

GRACE.   With her soft hand stroking my hair, and her dear eyes full of love and tenderness looking into mine, she said, "When you have gained a good man's love, cherish it, defend it; 'tis a woman's refuge in every trouble." And she loved you, father.

MORGAN.   Heaven knows she did. (*Aside.*) And she knew my story.

CAPTAIN (*outside*).   Moping in the cabin, with this glorious breeze on deck?

(*Enter* CAPTAIN, C.)

CAPTAIN.   How's this, how's this? We've cleared the point, set every inch of canvas; and the " Seabright " is just sliding through the water like the duck she is, and such a beauty! Man and boy I've sailed the sea for thirty years, and never saw her equal. Ah, you rich chaps may well be envied by the less fortunate, when money can set such skimmers of the sea afloat. Come, come on deck: you are losing a grand sight.

ARABELLA (*outside*).   Oh, save me, save me! (*Enters from* R., *her face and hair wet, her arms moving as in the act of swimming.*) Stop the ship! Stop the ship, I'm drowning! The water's pouring into my stateroom! Oh, save my trunk!

CAPTAIN.   You've been tampering with the port-hole. Just like a woman.

(*Exit into stateroom,* R. I.)

ARABELLA.   O Alvah, why did you drag me from home? Do you want to see me drown before your eyes? Have I lived forty — thirty years to meet a watery grave? Why don't somebody get out the lifeboat? We're all going to the bottom. (*Swims to companion-way, and is going up.*)

MORGAN (*bringing her back*).   Tut, tut, there's no danger.

(*Enter* CAPTAIN, R. I.)

CAPTAIN.   Not a bit. You opened the port as she was heeling to starboard, and a shower-bath was the natural consequence.

ARABELLA.   What! ain't we sinking?

CAPTAIN.   Bless you! no, my ships never sink.

ARABELLA.   Then I'll go back and hang up my wardrobe

to dry, but do keep her up straight, Captain. This heeling is awful sickening. (*Exit* R. I.)

MORGAN. So, Captain, you're one of the luckies. Never lost a ship?

CAPTAIN. Never; and only wrecked once.

MORGAN. When was that, Captain?

CAPTAIN. Long ago, a matter of eighteen years. We were running down from Melbourne to San Francisco, in the "Vulture."

MORGAN (*agitated.*) The "Vulture"?

CAPTAIN. One of the "Vultures." There are many afloat, but she, poor old gal, went to the bottom. I was afore the mast, and among my messmates was Jack Ober.

MORGAN (*agitated*). Ah, the old name!

CAPTAIN. Ah, poor old Jack! he turned out a bad lot, but we were cronies then. I remember sitting on the fo'castle rail with him many a moonlight night, spinning yarns of boyhood days. Poor old Jack! we were that fond of each other that we tattooed on our breasts, he on mine, I on his, the picture of a vulture — like this. (*Throws back his shirt, showing picture.* MORGAN *hastily fumbles with his as if to conceal something.*) We were ten days out when, in the middle watch, a cyclone struck us. Such a blow! The confusion was awful. The sea roaring over the ship, and banging against her sides, with concussions that made you think of the breaking-up of the world, the gale howling through the rigging like forty locomotive whistles in full blast, the night black as ink, the captain and mate howling at the top of their voices, and the ship on her beam-ends, and leaking like a sieve! We cut the boats adrift, and sought safety in that boiling caldron. There was one gold-digger, Martin Secor, who was returning with his little boy and a belt full of gold. With this man and the little chap, Jack and I left the ship in a cockle-shell of a boat. It was a tough fight for life, but we won. When the storm broke we found ourselves abreast a small island, where we made a landing. The little chap was nearly dead, but with careful nursing we brought him round ; and for three days we struggled for life on the few roots we dug from the soil. The father grew wild with anxiety for his boy: he would run along the shore, waving his money-belt heavy with gold, shouting for help, and offering "gold, gold, for bread." On the fourth morning I awoke to find the boat, Martin Secor, and my messmate Jack, gone. I was alone with the boy.

MORGAN. The father had deserted his child.

CAPTAIN. Do you believe that? Would any thing tempt me to desert my little Polly? Would any thing tempt you to desert your daughter? No, that's not the sort of timber that daddies are made of. It was a crafty trick of Jack Ober's. My messmate, whom I would have trusted with my life, had murdered the father, and escaped with the gold.

MORGAN (*agitated*). How did you learn this?

CAPTAIN. I guessed it. I know nothing of the fate of the father: I only know he loved his boy, and that Jack Ober deserted me, his messmate. Put this and that together, and think what you please. I have never seen Jack since; but justice is perfect, and somewhere in this world or the next we shall meet again, — for reckoning.

GRACE. And the boy?

CAPTAIN. That day we were taken off by a passing vessel. I fell into a raging fever, and for weeks was dead to thought and action. When I recovered I was in a hospital in San Francisco, and the boy was gone on the ship that rescued us. I could never find him.

GRACE. Poor fellow!

CARTER (*outside*). Captain Taylor ahoy! ahoy! ahoy! (*Appears coming down companion-way.*)

GRACE. Mr. Carter! I will not meet him. (*Exit*, L. I.)

CAPTAIN. Well, Mr. Carter, what's the matter?

CARTER. Will you overhaul your reckoning, and inform me where we are?

CAPTAIN. Three miles east of the Big Brewster.

CARTER. In deep water?

CAPTAIN. Very deep water.

CARTER. Then if you will kindly order up a hammock, load one end with shot, sew me up in it, and consign me to the mighty deep, you will place me under obligations for the rest of my existence, which, under the circumstances, must necessarily be limited.

CAPTAIN. What misfortune has befallen you?

CARTER. The worst: I've met a brother.

CAPTAIN. Ah, some long-lost relative?

CARTER. No such good fortune. A brother of the "Antique and Venerable Order of Disgruntled Growlers."

Pacing the deck of my own gallant craft, I have been accosted by one of your tarriest of tars, who, placing his left hand behind his left ear, extends his right hand, and whispers "Divy." He was a Growler.

MORGAN. And you?

CARTER. Oh, I'm his brother fast enough. I'm a "Growler," — I've been Grand Custodian of the Candidates, Grand Inspector of the Gridiron, Grand Keeper of the Goats, Grand Chamberlain of the Chowder-Bowl, Great Grand Panjowdah, grand every thing.

CAPTAIN. What is the object?

CARTER (*spouting, with upraised hand*). "The uplifting of the order of society by bombastic explosion, and the rebuilding from its shattered fragments a nobler system, which shall extend to the remotest corners of the earth, and whose towering battlements shall pierce the heavens." Bosh!

MORGAN. Then, you don't believe in it.

CARTER. Not much. Once I was its most devoted subject; that was when I was a thirsty-throated son of the street-corners. Then I knelt before its bucket of vermilion-dyed liquid, typical of human gore, and swore to be a true Terrific Disgruntled Growler until those vampires, the Jay Goulds, the Vanderbilts, and all the aristocrats of wealth, succumbed to our invincible war-cry, "Divy."

MORGAN. This was before your uncle died?

CARTER. Yes; when my venerable relative, commonly known as old miser Carter, shipped his cable, and sailed for a new harbor, he left to me, his only relative, a black trunk, packed with bonds of the X. Y. and Z. Railroad, stocks in the Don Quixote mine, and titles to rivers of oil. I hadn't the heart to growl, and no disposition to feel disgruntled, so I quietly shook the Antique Order; but the Antiques did not shake well. They were never such firm friends. They gathered about me with extended hands, and the Antique motto, "Divy," on their lips. I was invited to pour into their treasury my legacy. I did not accept. I was entreated to prove my principles. I quietly informed the special committee that I did not intend to disturb my principals, but to live upon my interests. Then they threatened me. Any brother had power to slay me at sight without grace; there was no escape but by compliance with the Antique rule, "Divy." I thought, when I sailed off in my own boat, I had buried the past; but there rises before me a ghost in sailor trousers who salutes me with the old story, "Divy." So, Captain, bring up your stoutest hammock, sew me up tight, and let me slide; the waters will "divy" to receive me, and society will have one "Growler" less.

CAPTAIN. Oh, no! we can't spare either you or the shot. So come on deck, point out your "brother," and you shall hear no more from him. (*Exit, companion-way.*)

MORGAN. Ha! ha! Carter, your troubles are serious. A millionnaire in deadly peril. I see but one way of escape for you.

CARTER. One is enough, I'll take it.

MORGAN. You must marry, settle all your wealth upon your wife. You will then be a poor man, and free. The "Growlers" cannot make war upon a woman. Look about you; we've good material here. There's the captain's daughter, pretty, but young; my sister, well, a little over the line; and my daughter, she might be induced to take pity on a martyr. Ha! ha! ha! ha! look about you, Carter, look about you. (*Exit* C.)

CARTER. Egad, the old gentleman is worse than the "brothers;" they would be satisfied with a fair division, he would *free* me of the whole. It's not the first time he has hinted that his daughter might be had for the asking. Now's my chance; she's beautiful and accomplished, and would make my ducats dance a merry measure.

(*Enter* CRUMBS, R. 1 E.)

CRUMBS (*creeping towards* CARTER *with his finger on his lips*). H'sh!

CARTER. What's the matter with you?

CRUMBS. Are we alone?

CARTER. Evidently.

CRUMBS. Sh! (*Puts left hand behind ear, extends right, and whispers hoarsely.*) "Divy."

CARTER. Another, and a black one!

CRUMBS. Sh! (*Aside.*) Dis chile don' lose any chances. (*Aloud.*) Sh! (*Creeps back and off* R.)

CARTER. "Oh for a lodge!" oh, bother the lodge!

(*Enter* GRACE, L.)

GRACE. If I could only get this letter into the pilot's hands without my father's knowledge. Ah, Mr. Carter!

CARTER. Miss Morgan, when an individual, neither handsome in person nor agreeable in manner, but burdened with riches, finds himself irresistibly attracted to a lady who is quite the opposite, and has her father's sanction, what course should he pursue?

GRACE (*aside*). The farce begins. (*Aloud.*) I hardly feel competent to give advice in such a case; but were you the individual and I the lady, I would have you say, "Madam, you are my guest, and during my stay you shall be treated with all respect."

CARTER. You shall be treated as a queen. Can you doubt it?

GRACE. Then I should say, "I have been hurried from my home, leaving behind one whom I dearly love."

CARTER. Ah! believe me, I did not know of this.

GRACE. One to whom I am engaged, who is to me the noblest of men; I have left him with no token, no — oh, Mr. Carter! I am in sore distress, I want a friend, a brother!

CARTER. A — a br — br — brother. (*Aside.*) Can she be a "Growler"?

GRACE. Here is a note I have written. If it could be placed in the hands of the pilot.

CARTER (*takes letter*). It shall be. (*Reads address.*) "Horace Gaylord," the young chap I met at your house?

GRACE. The same.

CARTER. Why, he's the prince of good fellows. A perfect smooth-faced brick. You have asked me to be a brother. I thought I hated that word, but you have given it a new sound, and I'll serve you with my whole heart.

GRACE. Oh, thank you! you are a true knight cut from the antique.

CARTER (*aside*). I wish I was cut from them. (*Aloud.*) I have no time to lose, the pilot must be leaving the yacht. For you and for your love command me, — heart, soul, and uncle Carter's money. (*Aside.*) So closes one of Alvah Morgan's three ways of escape. (*Exit* C.)

GRACE. I think I have thwarted my father's matrimonial scheme in that direction.

(*Enter* ARABELLA, R. I.)

ARABELLA. Come, Grace, help me on deck; I shall stifle in this place. Of all the outrageous pranks your father has cut up, this beats all. Every roll of the ship sets my heart a-palpitating, every pitch sends me on my knees: I've bumped my head, rasped my knees, and lost my temper.

GRACE. Oh, you will make an excellent sailor, aunt, and learn to love the water.

ARABELLA. I always did hate it; and I know I shall be drowned.

GRACE. Come on deck, and all your fears will vanish.

ARABELLA. Hold me tight. If I get another fall, I'll crawl into my berth, and never get out again.

(GRACE *takes her arm, and they go up companion-way.*)

ARABELLA. Oh, how her timbers do shiver! Poor thing! (*Exeunt* C.)

(WOLF *staggers from locker.*)

WOLF. Oh, my head! my head! I'd rather face the foul fiend, or throw myself into the sea, than endure another hour's torture in that trap. We must be fairly out to sea. (*Goes to companion-way, and listens.*) No, I hear the pilot's voice still! What's to be done? If I am found, they will send me ashore with the pilot. Ah, not that, not that! The hungry wolf in his hiding-place has sharp ears, and your secrets, my masters, are in his keeping. As you deal with him, so shall it be with you, — justice for justice. Ah, some one comes; I cannot go back; I will seek safety elsewhere, and trust to chance. (*Exit into state room* R. I. GRACE *and* ARABELLA *return.*)

ARABELLA (*speaking as she descends*). It's no use, Grace; that last tumble just upset me. I thought I was going straight to David Jones's lockup.

GRACE. Oh, you promise to become a first-rate sailor.

ARABELLA. I'm going straight to bed, and stay there. (*Exit* R. I.)

GRACE. I saw the pilot take the letter.

ARABELLA (*screams*). A man! a man! (*Enters.*) O Grace, there's a great horrid sailor under my bunk.

GRACE. Nonsense, aunt.

ARABELLA. I saw him. Help! help! help!

(*Enter* CARTER, C.)

CARTER. What's wrong?

ARABELLA. A man in my room. A great, horrid, live man!

CARTER. Ah! I'll have him out. (*Exit* R. I.) Ah, you rascal!

WOLF (*inside*). Let go my throat.

CARTER. Come out, come out.

WOLF. Off, off, I say!

(*Enter* WOLF *and* CARTER, *struggling.* CARTER *throws
him down* C., *and stands over him.*

CARTER. Now, who are you?

WOLF. Well, call me Wolf.

CARTER. What do you want here?

WOLF (*raising himself, and extending his hand.*) " Divy."

CARTER. Confound it! (Goes R.) The sea is full of
them. (WOLF *rises and stands* L. *Enter* CAPTAIN, C.)

CAPTAIN. Ah, a stowaway! we'll make short work of you,
my man. On deck, and into the pilot-boat, quick. (*Enter*
MORGAN, C. *Starts at sight of* WOLF. *Goes* R. GRACE
goes to him, and talks with him. ARABELLA *sits in chair* L.)

CARTER. That's right, captain; put him ashore.

CAPTAIN. Come on deck, my man.

WOLF. Say, Captain, don't be hard on a poor chap. My
ship's in Bermuda. I'll work my passage, only give me a
chance.

CARTER. Put him ashore.

WOLF (*reproachfully*). Brother!

CARTER. Oh, bother!

CAPTAIN. You must go.

WOLF (*goes up* C. *and turns.* CAPTAIN *goes* L.). You're
rough on an old salt; but it's the way of the ocean. You
wouldn't have found me here if I hadn't been cheated by
sailors. I had gold, heaps and heaps, but I was robbed, —
robbed by messmates, —robbed of my hard-won gold, robbed
of my boy.

CAPTAIN. Robbed? When? Where?

WOLF. In the Pacific, eighteen years ago.

MORGAN. Ah! I thought I knew that face.

WOLF (*fiercely*). You knew it?

MORGAN. No, no, I am mistaken.

CAPTAIN. Wrecked and robbed in the Pacific! What
ship, messmate?

WOLF. The "Vulture."

CAPTAIN. The "Vulture." Your name?

WOLF. Oh, I've a dozen. 'Tis Wolf here; 'twas Martin Secor there.

MORGAN. 'Tis he. (*Sinks into chair.*)

CAPTAIN.   Martin Secor!

CARTER.   Put him ashore, captain.

CAPTAIN.   No, no!

CARTER.   I say yes.   I am the owner of this craft.

CAPTAIN.   And I her captain.   'Tis the law of the sea, that the captain rules, and all obey, even the owner. (*Goes* C.)   I'll not go back on an old messmate with whom I've sailed and starved. (*Shakes* WOLF's *hand.*)   Martin Secor sails with us.

PICTURE.

R., MORGAN *in chair, his face turned away from* C.   CARTER, *standing by table.*   C., CAPTAIN *and* WOLF, *hands clasped.*   L., ARABELLA *in chair,* GRACE *with her hand on her shoulder.*

ACT II.—IN MID-OCEAN.

Cabin at night. Lamps lighted. CAPTAIN *seated at table* L. MORGAN *seated* R. CRUMBS *standing* C.

CAPTAIN. So, you rascal, you've been putting Phillis on short allowance.

CRUMBS. What, I, cap'n, I? Why, bress your soul, dat ar' gal am a regular hipperpotanuse, she'd debour a whale ef de oben was large 'nuff to cook it. Her appetite am like de widow Cruise's oil, it nebber gibes out. Ef she could hab a free pass fro' de bill ob fare, dar'd be noffin' fur de fust table. Oh, she — she's —

CAPTAIN. A nice girl, and shall have all she wants. So change your tactics, or we shall quarrel.

CRUMBS. Tactics? don't know dat dish. Got hard tack —

CAPTAIN. You know what I mean. Better fare and more of it.

CRUMBS. Say, cap'n, were you eber in lub?

CAPTAIN. What's that to do with eating?

CRUMBS. Oh, heaps. Ef you eber felt de tender passion, your experience must hab taught you dis, — de greater de strain on de digestive organs, de more de functions ob de heart am brought in play, causing de enlargement ob dat organ, an' de consequential outpouring ob affection.

CAPTAIN. Nonsense!

CRUMBS. Dat's so; but don't de poet say —

> "A leetle nonsense now and den
> Am relished by de wisest men."

Fur instance, you take your bes' girl out fur de prominade; de ebenin' am profishus, de air am sweet and balmy, the stars am shinin' lub, and you meander in bliss. But, jus' dar, de light from de ice-cream saloon obscures your path, de fair objec' ob your affection hangs heaby on your arm and feels faint. You take de hint and de girl in, and you order de frozen sweets, and she is happy wid dem, and forgets de odder sweet dat pays de bill. But if when you see dat light

23

you shoot by, takin' de girl widout de hint, dar's no conflictin' element to disturb de harmony, an' you sabes your money.

CAPTAIN. Are you in love with Phillis?

CRUMBS. Oh, don't I lub dat girl!

CAPTAIN. You Turk! you were to have been married on the night we sailed, to another.

CRUMBS. Why, dat was a week ago, cap'n. Don't de poet say —

       "'Tis absence makes de heart grow fonder"

ob somebody else. I'se only jes' train' Phillis down to de lovin' point, dat's all.

CAPTAIN. Now stop it, or I'll train you with a diet of rope's end. Now go.

CRUMBS. Ay, ay, sir! (*Goes* R. *aside*.) Dat settles it. Thus ends my dream ob lub. (*Exit* R. I E.)

CAPTAIN. The rascal! I hate to be deceived.

MORGAN. And yet you trust this stowaway "Wolf."

CAPTAIN. Martin Secor! Yes.

MORGAN. He's no more Martin Secor than I am. Just think of it, captain. The man was concealed somewhere about the cabin; he could easily have heard the story of the shipwreck as you told it the day we sailed. Nothing easier than to assume the character. He can tell the story glibly as far as you told it. Beyond that he knows nothing.

CAPTAIN. Poor fellow, the thought of it makes him wild. You know that since that night he has been in his stateroom most of the time, sick.

MORGAN. In your stateroom, which you gave up to him. Why not send him among the men, where he belongs?

CAPTAIN. An old messmate! I had not the heart to do it. Possibly you may be right in your suspicions; but, somehow, I have faith in Martin Secor.

MORGAN. Depend upon it, he is an impostor.

CAPTAIN (*rising*). He is doing no harm here.

MORGAN. He is a dangerous character, and I wish we were well rid of him. Can't he be put ashore somewhere?

CAPTAIN. Possibly, but not while I command here. I have said he shall sail with us, and I always keep my word. (*Exit* C.)

MORGAN (*rises, and comes* R.). Blind confidence. The presence of that man terrifies me: if he is Martin Secor, he should be at the bottom of the sea. (WOLF *slips in from door* L. 2, *and sits* L., *with arms folded.*) If he is not, he knows nothing that should cause alarm; and yet I fear him.

WOLF. " Martin Secor sails with us." The captain is true blue.

MORGAN (*turns*). You here?

WOLF. Yes, to confound you; you, the man of wealth, tortured with doubts and fears. Ho! ho! your pleasure trip is not all sunshine and gentle breezes. Cabin walls are thin, and listeners may hear both good and evil reports. Stanch and true the man of the sea, bitter and fierce the man of the world. Should I tell what I know —

MORGAN. What do you know?

WOLF. What I would not tell before that faithful soul who so dearly prized an unworthy messmate. With you 'tis different. You doubt me. (*Rises.*) Listen. When Jack Ober snatched my money-belt and took to the boat, I followed; too late to seize him ere he had embarked, maddened with the loss of my money, I sprang into the sea, and swam after the boat. 'Twas a hard pull, but I overtook him, seized the gunwale, and would have lifted myself into the boat ; but with an oath the fiend raised an oar, and struck me. I lost my hold, and sunk.

MORGAN (*aside*). 'Tis he. (*Sinks into chair* R. *Aloud.*) Well, go on.

WOLF. No; I've said enough, you doubt me no longer. I live only to meet Jack Ober to bring him to bay. When that time comes, he shall confess his crime. Of my past I have nothing to be ashamed. You would breed trouble between that heart of oak and the messmate he would befriend. You have an uneasy conscience that feeds on suspicion. Cover *your* record well, lest accident or design betray the secret of your life. Remember this, amid your doubts and fears: as truly as you are Alvah Morgan, I am Martin Secor of Melbourne. (*Exit* L. 2.)

MORGAN. And still I doubt. The blow was sure, the man sunk like lead, sunk to his death; else why this sickening feeling of guilt in spite of his story? (*Rises.*) Why, in the night, do I still wake in terror to see those pleading eyes fastened upon me? This man knows too much. He is indeed dangerous. Oh, if I could but blot out that bloody record? (*Sinks into chair.*)

(*Enter* GRACE L. I.)

GRACE. Why, father, are you ill?

MORGAN. No, no! I'm not so good a sailor as I was, and the motion of the vessel troubles me. 'Twill soon wear off.

GRACE. Have you been alone? I thought I heard voices.

MORGAN (*agitated*). What did you hear?

GRACE. Only a murmur. Who was with you?

MORGAN. Martin Secor.

GRACE. Who *is* Martin Secor, father?

MORGAN. An old friend of the captain.

GRACE. Have I ever met him before?

MORGAN. Not to my knowledge. Why?

GRACE. He acts so strangely. On deck he avoids me, when I speak to him, he looks out to sea, mutters, and turns away; but often I've seen him standing leaning against the foremast, with his eyes fixed upon my face, and once as I passed him, in the companion-way, he seized my hand and pressed it to his lips.

MORGAN. Did he dare?

GRACE. He acts very strangely.

MORGAN (*tapping his forehead*). Not quite right here. Avoid him.

GRACE. Poor old fellow. There's something on his mind that worries him. I hope he has committed no crime; that his conscience is —

MORGAN. How speeds Carter's suit?

GRACE. With Polly Taylor?

MORGAN. With Polly! I don't understand.

GRACE. Mr. Carter told me you had pointed out to him three ways of escape from some deadly peril, the first of which was marriage with Polly. I think he is trying that.

MORGAN. The donkey! Didn't I also tell him you might be had for the asking?

GRACE. Did you, indeed? how very kind! He knew better than to ask, after he found that I was engaged.

MORGAN. Who told him that?

GRACE. Ha, ha! my father's child.

MORGAN. My father's child is a fool.

GRACE. Ha, ha! father —

MORGAN. Don't be absurd. Richard Carter is a prize well worth any woman's winning.

GRACE. That's what I told Polly.

MORGAN. Oh, bother Polly!

GRACE. I think he will. She does not appear to be sensible of his intrinsic *market* value.

MORGAN. This cruise was arranged purposely to bring you together.

GRACE. Indeed! I thought it was to benefit my health.

MORGAN. I know he admires you. Smile upon him, and you will bring him and his millions to your feet.

GRACE. And break another man's heart. Thank you, no. Don't worry about me, father; Mr. Carter and I are the best of friends, and quite agreed, that, to use his own words, Horace Gaylord is the prince of good fellows.

MORGAN. Prince of humbugs! I've no patience with you. Not a penny of my money goes to enrich him, remember that. I'll leave it all to charity.

GRACE. As "charity begins at home," and I intend to keep him there, we shall share it together. Come, take me on deck.

MORGAN. The night is very dark, the wind fierce —

GRACE. And the sea running high; no matter, the mighty deep in any form delights me, and it's so beneficial to my health. Ha, ha! come along. (*Takes his arm.*)

MORGAN. On deck, then. (*Exeunt,* C.)

CRUMBS (*outside*). Here you, here you!

Enter PHILLIS *running from* R. I E., *with the leg of a turkey in her hand, followed by* CRUMBS. *He catches her by right wrist in* C.

Stop thief, stop thief! Why — why — it's Phillis.

PHILLIS. Jes' so, Mr. Crumbs, it's Phillis.

CRUMBS (*releasing her*). Wh— wh— what you doin' in de larder?

PHILLIS. Getting my supper. You don't suppose I was such a ninny as to submit to your low fare, do you? No, indeed, not for Phillis. While you have been trying to starve me into submission, I've been feasting on the enemy's stores. (*Holds up turkey.*)

CRUMBS. She boned de turkey, caught in de act. O Phillis! I blush for you.

PHILLIS. Don't strain your complexion on my account.

CRUMBS. Dat's whar all de provender disappeared, and I thought it was de rats. O Phillis, Phillis! de perfidy ob woman am past finding out.

PHILLIS. That's so. You don't set the right sort of trap. I've been living on the fat of the land.

CRUMBS. Yas, indeed; an' growin' plumper an' plumper ebery day. An' I thought de starbin' cure was jes' gwine to do de business.

PHILLIS. So your little scheme has failed. Eh, Mr. Crumbs?

CRUMBS. O Phillis! don't look at me in dat way. Dat's cruelty, — cruelty to animals. Oh! ef I was only dat turkey-leg, dat I might press dose lips. (*Approaches her.*)

PHILLIS. Stand off! turkey is nice, but I don't like goose.

CRUMBS. O Phillis! I'll forgib de rabagin' ob de larder, ef you'll only say you lub me.

PHILLIS (*nibbling turkey*). What, with my mouth full of turkey? that would not be proper. But I may say it some time.

CRUMBS. When's dat, Phillis?

PHILLIS. When the right man asks me. Good night, Mr. Crumbs. I don't love you, but I just adore your larder. (*Exit*, L. I.)

CRUMBS. Dar's anudder mitten flung, another turkey spoiled. I shall hab to put dat ar' bird onto de table wid one leg in de grabe, an' de cap'n will jes' raise a row. O Phillis! she lubs not me but de larder. I'll jes' lock up dat hated' ribal tight, so she don't get no more comfort dar. (*Exit* R. I E.)

(*Enter* C., POLLY *and* CARTER.)

POLLY. Nonsense, Mr. Carter!

CARTER. It's the truth, Polly; you are just the most fascinating nymph of the sea, I ever set eyes on.

POLLY. Then, because I am a nymph of the sea, as you are pleased to call me, I cannot leave my mother; I was born on the water. Dad and I have sailed together for ten years in storm and calm. I have climbed the rigging in the darkest night. I have taken an oar in the boat, when the men have sought in the wild storm to save life on shipwrecked vessels. I can take my trick at the wheel with the best of them. I know every rope and sail, every shift of the wind, every shade of the clouds. You ask me to leave all this to live in splendor, in carpeted halls and marble palaces, to be the wife of a nabob.

CARTER. That's just what I ask you. You shall do nothing but dress in the finest, dance with the gayest, ride with the swiftest. All that money can buy shall be yours. We will share — no, that's only another name for "Divy," — all that I possess shall be yours.

POLLY. Thank you, not for me. Dad's good old heart would break to lose me, his messmate on many a voyage. Why don't you try Grace Morgan?

CARTER. Ah—hm! I prefer you, Polly.

POLLY. And — shall I tell you the truth, Mr. Carter?

CARTER. The truth, Polly.

POLLY. You're just as good as you can be to make me this nice offer; but — but — I prefer another.

CARTER. The deuce you do! Who is the happy party?

POLLY. Oh! he knows nothing about it.

CARTER. Tell me who he is; I'll make him plump down on his knees before you.

POLLY. But I thought you loved me.

CARTER. What's the use, when you love another?

POLLY. I'm not quite sure —

CARTER. O Polly! if there's a doubt, give me the benefit of it.

POLLY. I'm not quite sure that he cares for me.

CARTER. He can't help it. I'd give a hundred thousand for his chance. (*Aside.*) Preferred stock is booming.

(*Enter* CAPTAIN, C.)

CAPTAIN. Polly, my girl, bring me my reefer.

POLLY. Ay, ay, dad! (*Exit* L. I.)

CAPTAIN. It's cutting up rough outside, Mr. Carter.

CARTER. I'm glad of it; misery loves company.

CAPTAIN. We're going to have a blow, a growler. Come on deck, it's glorious.

CARTER. Excuse me, captain. I've had a blow here, and you know I don't care to meet growlers.

CAPTAIN. Had a blow; what do you mean?

CARTER. I've been asking your daughter to marry me.

CAPTAIN. The deuce you have!

CARTER. But she's not inclined that way. It's all right, captain, nothing's broke. (*Aside.*) Thus ends another of Morgan's brilliant matrimonial schemes. (*Exit* R. 2.)

CAPTAIN (*whistles*). The nabob wants to marry my Polly, whew! My Poll — well, well; and she declines the honor, my Poll — a good man, Richard Carter: he can't sail a yacht, that's agin him; but he has good points, and would make Polly a capital husband.

(*Enter* POLLY, L. 1, *with reefer.*)

POLLY.   Here's your reefer, dad.

CAPTAIN (*sinks into chair* L.).   Polly, come here.

POLLY.   Ay, ay, dad. (*Kneels* L. *of his chair.*)

CAPTAIN.   Polly, my pet, you and I are old messmates.

POLLY.   Ay, ay, dad.

CAPTAIN (*smoothing her hair*).   Ay, ay! we've weathered many a storm together, shared many joys, and—and one great sorrow.

POLLY.   Ay, ay, dad.   Poor dear mother.

CAPTAIN.   You haven't forgotten that night in the Bay of Biscay?

POLLY.   No, dad; it would be impossible to forget that.

CAPTAIN.   The fever was too much for her, she could not rally.   I see her now, white and motionless, lying on the deck, as we slowly drifted.

POLLY (*sobbing*).   Dying, dad, dying!

CAPTAIN.   I don't like the word, Polly: I like to think of her as drifting out of a troubled sea into peaceful waters; for surely on her sight broke the headlands of the celestial harbor.   Ah, pretty one! she left her country home to follow my fortunes.   Happy always on the ocean.

POLLY.   Dear, dear mother!

CAPTAIN.   Her last thoughts were of you, her last words —

POLLY.   " Never desert your father."   I remember, dad; it was but a whisper, but I have never forgotten it. (*Sobbing.*) O dad, dad! in all the wide world there is no one so good and true as you.   I shall cling to you as long as I live.

CAPTAIN (*hugging her*).   Now, now, don't fret, my pet; don't fret.   Now, Polly, tell me, tell me true, was that the reason you refused Mr. Carter?

POLLY.   Why, dad, who told you?

CAPTAIN.   Mr. Carter, the enormously wealthy Mr. Carter!   Not a bad man, Polly.   Such chances for shipping on the voyage of life are scarce.   If you care for him, Polly, don't let thought of me stand in the way of your happiness. Of course I shall miss my little shipmate.   I may feel a bit lonesome sometimes, and — and — mother won't care (*wiping his eyes*) if you are happy.

POLLY. You dear old dad, I don't care one bit for Mr. Carter, and I do not want to marry him.

CAPTAIN. You don't? Give us a hug. Then it's all right.

POLLY. Mother told me once that if I wanted to be happy, to marry a sailor.

CAPTAIN (*whistles*). Bless her dear heart, did she? I never heard of it.

POLLY. It was one of her secrets. I shall take her advice. Of course, I shall never get such a grand one as she did.

CAPTAIN. Polly, my pet, you're getting tangled in your tongue tackle.

POLLY. So I shall content myself with a common sailor.

CAPTAIN. All right, Polly, one of these days.

POLLY. Dad, do you think Tom Tucker will make a good sailor?

CAPTAIN. What! that green gosling, that land-lubber, who's in everybody's way, he? He doesn't know the martingale from the gaub-line.

POLLY. Did you, the first time you went to sea?

CAPTAIN. No; but I didn't ship as an able seaman.

POLLY. But he can learn, can't he?

CAPTAIN (*whistles*). Polly, my pet, it seems to me you take uncommon interest in this uncommon seaman. What's Tom Tucker to you?

POLLY. Why, nothing, of course; but he's young and, and —

CAPTAIN. Polly Taylor! I'm afraid I've been foolish in allowing you to repel Mr. Carter.

POLLY. Oh, no, dad! oh, no!

CAPTAIN. It looks as though a storm was brewing in another quarter. I'll keep my eye on Master Tom Tucker. (*Rises.*) Give me my reefer, I must go on deck. Good-night, pet. (*Kisses her.*)

POLLY. Good-night, dad.

CAPTAIN. Turn in early. (*Exit* C.)

POLLY. Ay, ay, dad. The thought of my miraculous escape from becoming a fine lady is evidently troubling dad. 'Twas rather selfish in me, for I could have given dad a ship, and made Tom Tucker, — no, I couldn't make any thing of Tom with Mr. Carter's money; but I've set the captain to thinking, and I shouldn't wonder if Master Tom's chances of becoming a sailor improved. Ha, ha! there's plenty of room, he's such a blunderhead. (*Exit* L.)

TEDDY (*creeping down companion-way*). I wonder where Martin Secor bunks? Nice old chap, Martin; he seems to have taken a particular fancy to me, and helps me over lots of hard places; he's not been on deck to-night, I'm afraid he's sick. I wonder which is his room? I'll try this. (*Knocks at door* L. 1; POLLY *appears*.)

POLLY. Well, what is it? Good gracious! Tom Tucker.

TEDDY. Ay, ay! beg pardon, I thought 'twas Secor's room.

POLLY. Next door.

TEDDY. Thank you, Miss Tucker. (*Turns away.*)

POLLY. Ahem! Found that friend yet?

TEDDY. What friend?

POLLY. That was to formally present you to me.

TEDDY. How can I when you've forbidden me to try?

POLLY. I'm afraid Cy Goodwin will get ahead of you.

TEDDY. Afraid! Well, that's consoling. Why?

POLLY. Dad trusts him with the wheel, and that often brings him near me.

TEDDY. Cy's luck! "Dad" never trusts me with any thing.

POLLY. That's because you're a bad sailor.

TEDDY. I suppose I am a pretty shabby lot in the nautical line. I'm a stunner at baseball, football, and other collegiate studies; but I'd rather be a sailor than any thing else.

POLLY. We are always wanting the impossible; but why wish to be a sailor?

TEDDY. To be always near you.

POLLY. That would be nice.

TEDDY. O Polly!

POLLY. If you were a sailor. As you are not, you will be obliged to keep your distance; that is nice too.

TEDDY. Thank you, Miss Tucker. I'll try. (*Turns away.*)

POLLY. Better give your attention to seamanship. You don't know the sails or the ropes. I don't believe you can make a long splice.

TEDDY. I can learn.

POLLY. When?

TEDDY. After the introduction.

POLLY. Not with my help.

TEDDY. With yours and a minister's.

POLLY. You don't understand. A long splice is some-thing belonging to a ship.

TEDDY. I know, courtship too. In either case 'tis the end of a rope.

POLLY. Which you richly deserve.

TEDDY. Thank you for your good wishes.

POLLY. You will never succeed.

TEDDY. Oh, you don't know me.

POLLY. Yes, I do; you're a fresh, — a fresh-water sailor.

TEDDY. Bound to rise. You know the immortal Daniel once said, " There is always room at the top."

POLLY. You'll never reach it, you can't climb the rigging. You can do nothing.

TEDDY. I can love you.

POLLY. Without an introduction? Oh, no! Mr. Tucker. You're too forward. Go where you belong.

TEDDY. That's forward.

POLLY. Sir!

TEDDY. In the fo'castle, you know.

VOICE (*outside*). All hands on deck. Ahoy! ahoy! ahoy!

POLLY. There, you're wanted, and you're keeping me out of my berth.

VOICE (*outside*). Tumble up, tumble up!

POLLY. That means you! That's where you excel.

TEDDY. In what, please?

POLLY. Tumbling, ha, ha! you a sailor! Oh, my! Heaven help me if my life was placed in your keeping. Ha, ha! (*Exit* L. I.)

TEDDY. She's just jolly. She may laugh at me now; but as the venerable chestnut says, "let those laugh who win," and I'm bound to beat Cy Goodwin. Now for a word with Secor. (*Knocks.*)

WOLF (*outside*). Come in.

TEDDY. Ay, ay! messmate. (*Exit door* L. 2.)

MORGAN (*outside*). Thank you, captain. If you will keep an eye on Grace, I'll go below.

CAPTAIN (*outside*). Ay, ay!

(*Enter* MORGAN, C.)

MORGAN. I cannot stay on deck; the roaring blast of the

gale fans the unrest which the words of Martin Secor have created. Martin Secor, Martin Secor! that name throbs in my brain, I cannot banish it,—the man I doubt, and yet dread. Oh, why does he haunt me! While he lives there is no peace for me. If he were dead — dead — dead — 'twould be an easy matter to enter his stateroom in the night, rid myself. No — no — what ideas pursue me! I murder? I — no, no, no more of that. (*Exit* R. 2; *enter* TEDDY L. 2.)

TEDDY. He's all right, says he's coming on deck; nice old chap, insisted on my taking his sou-wester because it's going to be a rough night. (*Puts on "sou-wester."*) There's Polly's door. I wonder if it would be safe to knock, and say "good-night." No, I'll not venture, it might be dangerous. (*Exit* C.; *as he goes up companion-way, enter* MORGAN, R. 2.)

MORGAN. Martin Secor again! he's going on deck for his nightly prowl. What a chance! A push at the head of the companion-way, and he is in the sea, where he belongs; 'tis too good a chance to lose. (*Darts up* C., WOLF *enters* L. 2.)

WOLF (*close to locker, so as not to be seen by* MORGAN). That was Morgan. What new mischief —

VOICE (*outside*). Man overboard, man overboard!

MORGAN (*rushes down* C.). I took the chance, and won. (*Exit* R. 2.)

WOLF. Foul play, I'll swear. (*Darts up* C.; *tumult outside, trampling of feet, rattling of chain, voices shouting* "*Fling a rope!*" "*Lower away the boat!*" "*There he is!*")

(*Enter* GRACE, C.)

GRACE. Oh, I cannot bear the sight!

(*Enter* POLLY, L. I.)

POLLY. What's the trouble now?

GRACE. A man overboard, struggling for life in the mad sea. O Polly, such a sight!

POLLY. Is dad on deck?

GRACE. Yes.

POLLY. Then the man is saved. My dad never deserts sailors in distress on land or sea.

GRACE. But there's another. No sooner had the cry been raised, "Man overboard," than a man rushed by me and threw himself into the sea. (*Enter* CARTER, R. 2.)

CARTER. Have we sprung a leak, run ashore, or collided?
I haven't heard so much noise since I took the one hundred
and ninety-first degree of Growlers.

VOICES (*outside*). Hurrah, hurrah, they've got 'em!

CARTER. I should think they had, bad.

(*Enter* CAPTAIN, C.)

CAPTAIN. We're all right, the boy is safe.

POLLY. What boy, dad?

CAPTAIN. The boy that's always in mischief; your *miserable* seaman, Tom Tucker.

POLLY. O dad, is he safe? Where is he? O dad, Tom
Tucker!

CARTER (*aside*). Ha, ha! preferred stock.

CAPTAIN. Safe, the rascal! to be sure he is. But it was
a narrow squeak for the boy. Ah, Carter! one of your
" Growlers " has covered himself with glory.

CARTER. Is it possible?

CAPTAIN. Here they come, the boy and his preserver.

(*Enter* C., WOLF *with his arm around* TEDDY.)

WOLF. Look up, lad, you are safe. (*Leads him to chair*
L. TEDDY *sinks into it, and closes his eyes.*)

TEDDY (*faintly*). I can't swim another stroke.

POLLY (*at L., strokes his hair*). Tom, Tom! look up, you're
safe.

CARTER (*to* WOLF). Brother, your hand. (*They shake.*)
How's this? You don't give the grip.

WOLF (*smiling*). You're not in position.

CARTER. Faith, he's right; but " Growler" or no
" Growler," command me for the half of my inheritance.

WOLF (*holds out his hand*). " Divy."

CARTER. Oh! that hateful word again. (*Comes* R.)

TEDDY. My head swims, and I'm as weak as a rat.

POLLY. Run and get some brandy, dad.

TEDDY. No, no! I'll come round all right. Say, Martin,
who is the lady whose sweet voice falls so soothingly on my
ears?

WOLF. The captain's daughter.

TEDDY. I should like to know her; introduce me, please.

WOLF. Certainly. — Miss Taylor, it gives me pleasure to
introduce my friend Teddy Morgan.

POLLY. Teddy Morgan!

TEDDY (*jumping up*). Yours truly. Delighted to make

your acquaintance. Hooray! I've beat Cy Goodwin, and won the wager; I've been soused in the sea, and must be a regular salt, glory enough for one day. (*Dances about stage.*) Hip, hip, hooray! (*Dances up, and meets* MORGAN, *who enters from* R. I.)

MORGAN. Teddy Morgan, my son!

TEDDY (*falling back to chair*). My dad.

CAPTAIN. Your son! how came he on board the "Sea-bright"?

MORGAN. Let him answer that.

TEDDY. In good time, dad. I am more anxious to know how I came in the water.

CAPTAIN. Tumbled over, of course; I've been expecting it.

TEDDY. Wrong, captain; I don't tumble that way. I was pushed into the sea. Perhaps hurled would better express the manner in which I was treated, for 'twas a strong arm that sent me over.

MORGAN (*aside*). Wretch that I am! I've tried to drown my own boy. (*Sinks into chair* R.)

CAPTAIN. Who could have been guilty of so dastardly a deed?

POLLY. Could Cy Goodwin?

TEDDY. No, Polly. I beg pardon, Miss Taylor; Harvard fellows don't settle bets in that way.

CAPTAIN. I'll not sleep until I have discovered the wretch.

WOLF. Don't trouble yourself, captain. Take your rest in peace, be sure his sin will find him out.

MORGAN. Who spoke then?

CAPTAIN. Martin Secor; the man in whom I have faith, the man who at the peril of his life saved your son from a watery grave.

MORGAN. Martin Secor! (*Rises.*) He saved my boy? No; 'tis false, he's at the bottom of the sea; you are deceiving me. Oh, heavens! (*Falls.*)

WOLF. 'Tis only a faint. (*Raises his head to his knee. Throws back the collar of his shirt, showing the picture of a vulture on his breast. To* CAPTAIN.) Look there.

CAPTAIN (*extreme* L.). Gracious heavens! What do I see?

WOLF. The indelible prick of the sailor's needle. The years come and go, the old ship lies rotting at the bottom of the sea, but the vulture still lives (*points to figure*) there.

CAPTAIN. Jack Ober! my messmate.

PICTURE.

WOLF *with left hand holding back the collar of* MORGAN'S *shirt, right hand pointing to figure on his breast.* CAPTAIN *extreme* L., *pointing to* MORGAN. CARTER *extreme* L., *with arms folded.* POLLY *at table.* TEDDY *in chair,* L., *leaning towards* MORGAN *as if about to rise.*

ACT III.—IN PORT.

Cabin by daylight. CRUMBS *on his knees before* PHILLIS, *clasping her right hand.*

PHILLIS (*endeavoring to release her hand*). Mr. Crumbs, let me go.

CRUMBS. O Phillis, listen to de beating ob dis swelled heart! 'Tis yer last chance: take me now, or lose me for-ebber. In an hour we shall be anchored: we shall go ashore.

PHILLIS. And the first girl you meet, you will fall in love with.

CRUMBS. Dat's a fac; dat's what skeers me. I knows my weakness. Sabe from de temptations ob de fair sex.

PHILLIS. La, Mr. Crumbs, I 'spect I shall have to marry you to get rid of you!

CRUMBS. Dat's a fac; get rid of me, or I shall get rid of myself, by frowing this lub-lacerated body into de waters ob oblivion. Ef I can't lib wid you, I won't lib widout you. Sabe me, or be forebber haunted by de ghost ob a diseased African.

PHILLIS. Well, Mr. Crumbs, if you are of the same mind when we drop anchor, I'll consent —

CRUMBS. To marry me?

PHILLIS. To your becoming a ghost.
(TEDDY *runs down* C.)

TEDDY. Great Scott! (*Turns, and runs up* C. PHILLIS *screams, and runs off* L. I.)

CRUMBS (*rises*). Now, who's dat disturbin' de meetin'? In de bery moment ob excruciatin' bliss de spoiler comes, and Phillis scoots. (TEDDY *creeps down* C., *cautiously*.) Oh, it's you, young ham-boner!

TEDDY. I say, Crumbs, is the coast clear?

CRUMBS. Don't know nuffin bout de coast: de girl am cleared.

TEDDY. Sorry to have disturbed your *tête-a-tête.*

CRUMBS. Now don't you be calling names. She's Phillis, simple Phillis.

TEDDY. Simple! Do you think so, Crumbs? How about the larder?

CRUMBS. Now — now — who — who — Look a-here, young ham-boner! I don't want no nonsense. Dar ar chords in de human breast dat can't be handled wid impurity.

TEDDY. I've an idea that the fair Phillis has made as sad havoc with your chords as she did with your larder.

CRUMBS. Now — now —

TEDDY. Let's drop anatomy, and turn to business. Here's a letter for you. (*Presents letter.*)

CRUMBS (*taking it*). Letter for me? Whar did it come from?

TEDDY. A boat has just arrived from shore bringing the mail, which arrived on the steamer a week ago.

CRUMBS (*turning it over and over*). Who's it from?

TEDDY. Open it and see. Have you lost your senses?

CRUMBS. Los' my specs overboard de day we sailed: dat's what's de marter.

TEDDY. Shall I open it?

CRUMBS (*giving letter*). Ef you please.

TEDDY (*opens letter*). It's signed "Nicodemus Johnson."

CRUMBS. Dat so? Why, dat's de parson dat was about to jine Sophia Sassafras and me when de cyclone struck and dissolbed de caucus. What's he say?

TEDDY (*reads*). "Cornbrake Crumbs, Esq."

CRUMBS. Dat's me. Go on.

TEDDY (*reads*). "In de far distant country to which you are trabellin' dar are temptations."

CRUMBS. Dat's what I tole Phillis.

TEDDY (*reads*). "I know your weakness."

CRUMBS. An' I knows de parson's, — Welsh rarebits at two in de mornin', an soft-shell crabs dat make hard-shell sermons.

TEDDY (*reads*). "Dis is to warn you. When you axed me to rehearse wid you and Miss Sassafras de ceremony in de back parlor before de regular performance in de front, when you two jined right hands and spoke de words I told you, you were legally married " —

CRUMBS. Yas; well, I guess not: wa'n't no witnesses.

TEDDY (*reads*). "For de widow Sassafras was behind de door, and Welcome Jones was peekin' fro the keyhole."

CRUMBS. Dat settles it.

TEDDY (*reads*). "You are a married man; so behave yourself, and send my fee by return mail."

CRUMBS. Send de fee! Don't get no half-dollar fer a rehearsal from dis chile.

TEDDY. Accept my congratulations, Crumbs. (*Gives letter.*) Kiss the bride for me when you meet. The parson, the widow, and peeping Jones have settled you for life. Oh, happy, happy Crumbs! ha, ha, ha! (*Exit* C., *laughing.*)

CRUMBS (*mocking*). Haw, haw, haw! Dat ar ham-boner jes' make me wild. Wh — wh — what de widder Sassafras doin' ahind dat door? An' — an' dey call dat foolishness a weddin': 'spect I'se fixed, do; ain't no goin ahind de returns. But I guess ef de parson wants his fee, he'll hab to take it outer de contribution-box.

(*Enter* PHILLIS, L. I.)

PHILLIS. Oh! Mr. Crumbs, I've been thinking about your offer, and have decided that I — I — will accept you.

CRUMBS. What's dat?

PHILLIS. I am ready to marry you.

CRUMBS. Golly, here's a row! Must I shatter de proud hopes ob dat trusting girl? (*Aloud.*) O Phillis! my heart bleeds for you, but it must not, cannot, be. De surgeon hab jes' inform me dat I hab an enlargement ob de cattapillary glands which any excitement would precipitate into conglomoration ob de exotic nerbs.

PHILLIS. Then we will have a very quiet wedding: just the parson and a couple of witnesses.

CRUMBS. One ahind de door, and one ahind de keyhole. No, Phillis, no rehearsal.

PHILLIS. Rehearsal?

CRUMBS. Yes. Well, I mean, Phillis, it's no use knockin' at de door ob dis heart, for when de cattapillary glands am leadin' de orchestra in de grand harmony ob de human structure, de heart must play de second fiddle.

PHILLIS. Then you don't mean to marry me.

CRUMBS. I can't, Phillis. De parson — I mean de surgeon —

PHILLIS. Bother the surgeon! You've had a letter from home, from that Sassafras girl, and you want to throw me over. You base, deceitful man! (*sobs*) win a poor girl's love (*sobs*), and then basely (*sobs*) desert her! (*Sobbing.*)

CRUMBS. I feel for you, Phillis. I know what a loss I must be to you, but de will ob de medical surgeon must be obeyed.

PHILLIS (*sobbing*). Oh, what shall I do? what shall I do?

CRUMBS (*aside*). Now jes' see de harm dat comes ob rehearsals! Ef I jes' had dat Welcome Jones by de scruff ob de neck, I'd put his head fro' de smalles' keyhole ebber made.

PHILLIS (*sobbing*). O, Mr. Crumbs, do not forsake me!

CRUMBS. I'se sorry for you, Phillis, but de course ob true lub nebber did run smoove; an'—an'—I mus' run an' take a pill. (*Exit* R. 1 E.)

PHILLIS (*sobs until* CRUMBS *is off, then looks up smiling*). Take your pill, Mr. Crumbs. The surgeon that made it is well rid of you; ha, ha, ha! (*Exit* L. 1.)

ARABELLA (*sticks her head out* R. 1). I do believe this pesky boat is getting into smooth water again. (*Creeps out.*) For twelve days I've been tossed and tumbled in that narrow bunk, expecting every minute to be my last; and they call this a pleasure-trip. I've shrunk so I can scarcely keep my clothes from slipping off. Oh, dear! why did I leave my happy home?

(*Enter* CARTER, C.)

CARTER. Why, Mrs. Caraway, this is a surprise. Old Father Neptune has treated you so shamefully, we feared we should never see you again. But you are all right now?

ARABELLA. All there is left of me. Father Neptune has indeed treated me shamefully, ah! but not so badly as I was treated by one Richard Carter ten years ago.

CARTER. You allude to our little flirtation —

ARABELLA. Little flirtation! hear the man! The man to whom I gave my youthful affections, the man I worshipped as he sat enthroned among his fellows, the Grand Panjodah of the Antique Order of Disgruntled Growlers. Oh, those days, those happy, too happy days!

CARTER. But, my dear Arabella, those days have passed. You became the wife of old Tom Caraway, and I am no longer a Growler.

ARABELLA. Not a Growler? Have you basely deserted the craft that honored you? Have you forgotten those fiery terms which from your eloquent lips made tyrants of trade tremble, aristocrats of wealth quake?

CARTER. I've no occasion to remember them now. I'm rich. When a man's wealthy, he can't go round begging an excited multitude to "down with the rich." He might as well try to pull himself up by his boots.

ARABELLA. And for this man's sake I too became a Growler!

CARTER. What?

ARABELLA. I am a member of the Oriental Annex.

CARTER. Is it possible? Give me a sign.

(ARABELLA *places her left hand under her right elbow, the right hand upright, then slowly lets the hand fall forward three times.*)

CARTER. The sign of the spinster degree. Correct. What does it signify?

ARABELLA. That my hand is free.

CARTER. Correct. Now, then, the grip (*extends his right hand*) when a brother offers his hand.

ARABELLA (*extending her hand*). 'Nuff —

CARTER. Said —

BOTH (*clasping hands*). Shake.

CARTER. Correct. Now, then, the grand union sign.

ARABELLA. In position?

CARTER. Of course. (*They place themselves back to back.*) Now: one, two, three. (*They turn, embrace, and speak in each other's ear.*) "Divy."

TEDDY (*rushes down* C.). More spoons! (*Runs up* C.; ARABELLA *screams, and runs off*, R. I.)

CARTER (*looking after* TEDDY). Correct. The fair Arabella is undoubtedly a sister of the Oriental Annex of expectant tarryers, whose motto is "the good time coming." The good time does not come to all of them, but they have a good time hoping, all the same.

ARABELLA (*sticks her head out*). Are you alone?

CARTER. Correct. Enter, fear not.

ARABELLA (*enters*). Oh, what a misfortune to be caught in such a predicament!

CARTER. Never mind, Arabella: 'twas only a grand union sign.

ARABELLA. Who was the intruder?

CARTER. I didn't see his face; but as there's but one individual who is always round when he's not wanted, I should say it was Teddy Morgan.

ARABELLA. My nephew! The whole family will hear of it. I shall be laughed at.

CARTER. Not on my account. That little touch of the antique has rekindled the flame of love in the breast of the apostate Growler. You were my first, my only love. We have both sought the mysteries, have both knelt before the vermilion, both taken the vows. I've broken mine, but you are still among the faithful. Let us together seek the antique fane, and go into business together, with the grand union sign above the door.

ARABELLA. Mercy sakes! what are you talking about?

CARTER. About marriage.

ARABELLA. Oh!

CARTER. Will you have me?

ARABELLA (*quick*). Yes.

CARTER. Correct. Spinster sign for the last time, when a brother offers his hand. (*Extends his.*)

ARABELLA (*extending hers*). 'Nuff —

CARTER. Said —

BOTH. Shake.

ARABELLA. O Richard, I'm so happy!

CARTER. In future we'll be happy together. I'll go back to the antique, when I marry you. I'll give up my wealth.

ARABELLA. To whom?

CARTER. The Growlers, of course.

ARABELLA. Oh, no, my dear! you'll do nothing of the sort: we are aristocrats now.

CARTER. Do you intend to shake the Growlers too?

ARABELLA. All but one, when we are married. I may shake him if he does not behave himself.

CARTER. Correct. Arabella, I've seen younger women —

ARABELLA. Richard!

CARTER. Than Polly Taylor; handsomer women —

ARABELLA. Richard!

CARTER. Than the celebrated Jersey Lily —

ARABELLA (*tenderly*). O Richard!

CARTER. But for solid happiness and enduring bliss, give me the woman who dared join a mystic society, and keep its secret. These are belles, but she (*opening his arms*) — Arabella.

ARABELLA (*her arms about his neck*). My Grand Pan-jodah! (*Exeunt C.*)

(*Enter* WOLF, L. 2.)

WOLF. This masquerade is almost past endurance. For six days Jack Ober has kept his berth. Since that stormy night in mid-ocean no one has seen his face, except his daughter. They told me he was ill, nigh unto death. Have I gone too far? Have I racked this guilty man's conscience beyond the point of justice? Have I, in seeking to bring him to confession, been guilty of as foul a crime as that for which he suffers? No, no, I do but seek the fulfilment of a dying man's last request. Let me but meet him again, let but one penitential tear drop from his eyes, and the future is bright with hope. (*Enter* GRACE R. 2.) His daughter! (*Turns away, and, during the scene with* GRACE, *keeps his face from her.*)

GRACE. Martin Secor! The very man I hoped to meet!

WOLF. Your father is recovering?

GRACE. Thanks to a strong constitution, yes.

WOLF. I am glad to hear it.

GRACE. That is false. For every pang he has suffered, you have hugged yourself in triumph.

WOLF. I?

GRACE. Yes, you, a human vampire draining the life-blood of your victim! You have pursued him with relentless hate. In his delirium there was but one name on his lips, — Martin Secor. I hate the name as I hate you.

WOLF (*agitated, aside*). Heaven help me to bear this!

GRACE. How has my father wronged you? tell me, his daughter. Can gold requite? It shall be thrown to you in thousands. Must life alone satisfy your vengeance? Take mine: I would gladly die to save him. Speak! What is the wrong?

WOLF. I cannot answer you.

GRACE. Coward! you dare not. In some crafty way you have obtained some hold upon him. You are not bold enough to strike one blow, and free him from your power, but, vulture-like, feed on his fears, exulting in the prolongation of his misery. Oh, would that I were a man! I'd match my strength against your cunning. To a wretch like you, gray hairs should be no protection.

WOLF (*with an effort*). Lady, you wrong me: I am not the guilty wretch you think me. As freely as you would lay down your life for your father, would I mine for you and yours. If your father has wronged me, three words from his lips would be ample satisfaction : three little words worth more to me than gold or life ; for they would free me from an oath, free me from the taunt of cowardice, which from a fair woman's lips to an honest man, *which I am,* is worse than death.

GRACE. How is this? Have I been mistaken?

WOLF. Time will show. We are nearing port. Already the perfume of Bermuda's tropical luxuriance is wafted on the breeze. Ere your foot touches the land, you shall confess that Martin Secor is as true as yonder lover, who, across the sea, awaits tidings from his mistress. Only give me time. I'm old and weak, but, thank Heaven! neither wretch nor coward. (*Agitated.*) No, no! (*Staggers into* L. 2.)

GRACE. An honest man! His acts belie his words. He never looked me in the face. Three words would free him! If that is all, my father shall speak them. Capt. Taylor's words, " I have faith in Martin Secor," ring in my ears. I have no faith, but hope our voyage ended we shall see the last of Martin Secor.

(*Enter* POLLY, C.)

POLLY (*sings as she enters*).

> " A Yankee yacht and a Yankee crew,
>   Tally-i-o, you know,
>   Can beat the world on the waters blue ;
>   Sing hey aloft and alow."

Grace, we're nearly in. You should be on deck. Mrs. Caraway is there.

GRACE. Aunt on deck! that's good news.

POLLY. I'm afraid she's not feeling very well, for Mr. Carter has his arm around her, and she clings to him awfully. Are you going up?

GRACE. Not just now. I must go to my stateroom and look after Phillis. (*Exit* L. 1.)

POLLY. She's real nice. Of course : isn't she Ted's sister? Poor fellow! I snub him every time I have a chance, but I shall hate awfully to lose him. (*Turns to* C. *as* TEDDY *comes down, tumbling into her arms.*)

TEDDY. I beg pardon.

POLLY. Will you never learn to come down properly?

TEDDY. Don't want to, Miss Polly. The captain told me that if I continued to improve my chances I should succeed in breaking my neck; and I'm bound to succeed in something. Jolly lark on deck! Mr. Carter and aunt Arabella are spooning like Romeo and Juliet.

POLLY. Well, what of it?

TEDDY. It's shameful at their time of life. Mr. Carter is no chicken; and aunt Arabella, — well, she says she has seen our century-plant bloom once, and I know it's nearly ready to flower again.

POLLY. Why, Teddy Morgan! that would make her nearly a hundred years old. •

TEDDY. She looks it. Oh, she's fishing for him. I heard her call him her grand pan of chowder. Bah! and he looks at her, — well, I couldn't begin to describe the ecstatic gleams he manages to flash through his gig-lights!

POLLY. Oh, I know! Mrs. Caraway is not the only one who has received those tokens of affection. I wouldn't have believed the man could have so soon forgotten me.

TEDDY. You, Polly?

POLLY. Yes, me. I had only to say yes, and become a millionnairess.

TEDDY. What did you say?

POLLY. That I preferred another.

TEDDY. One Teddy Morgan, alias Tom Tucker, alias Ted the Fresh.

POLLY. Well, I like that.

TEDDY. Of course you do. You may snub Thomas Tucker as much as you please, but when Teddy Morgan, at the ripe age of twenty-one, says to you, "Polly, my darling, the parson is waiting for the bride and groom to make a long splice," you're not going to drop your end of the rope.

POLLY. I'm going to marry a sailor.

TEDDY. So you shall, Polly. I have burned my college-boats, and henceforth old ocean is my alma mater. In the words of a celebrated marine poet, "I'm bound to be a sailor-boy, by jingo! or die."

POLLY. Your father will never consent.

TEDDY. No matter as long as yours does. So give me your hand, my jolly little messmate (*takes her hand and kneels*), and hear me swear —

POLLY. Why, Ted!

TEDDY. That until this battered hulk lies bleaching on the shores of time, Teddy Morgan, able seaman —

POLLY. Ha, ha, ha!

TEDDY. Will be true to the sailor's toast, —

> "The wind that blows, the ship that goes,
> And the lass that loves a sailor."

How's that for nautics?

POLLY. Very good. You deserve promotion. You'll soon be able to command a smack, perhaps.

TEDDY (*throws arm about her waist*). I'd rather beg one.

POLLY (*struggling*). Teddy Morgan!

(*Enter* CAPTAIN, C.)

CAPTAIN. Belay, there, belay! (TEDDY *and* POLLY *separate, she over to* R., *he to* L.) You young pirate! what do you mean by boarding my little clipper in that way?

TEDDY. Well, you see, captain, she was running free, and I hove down to speak her, when my fore-yard arm got entangled in her waist, and —and —

CAPTAIN. Avast, you've unshipped your rudder. Polly, what new caper has this young lobster been cutting up?

POLLY. Nothing much, dad. He was running down, and I was running up, and we ran smack against each other.

TEDDY (*aside*). I missed the smack.

CAPTAIN. A pretty yarn! There's been too much skulking here. I don't like it. As soon as we anchor, Master Ted, I shall discharge you, and turn you over to your father.

TEDDY. But I don't like being turned over. I shipped for the voyage out and back. Why should you discharge me? I've done nothing.

CAPTAIN. Right, my lad; that's reason enough.

TEDDY. Very well, then, I shall ship on another vessel.

POLLY. And so will I.

CAPTAIN. Polly!

POLLY. He wants to be a sailor, and I want to have him —

TEDDY. After I become a sailor. Don't you see?

CAPTAIN. I see breakers ahead. On deck, you young rascal, and swab out the jolly-boat!

TEDDY. Ay, ay, sir! (*Goes up* C. *Turns in companionway.*) Polly, don't give up the ship.

CAPTAIN (*roars*). Will you be off?

TEDDY. Ay, ay, sir! (*Exit* C.)

CAPTAIN. Now, Polly Taylor, you're to have nothing more to do with that young porpoise.

POLLY. Ay, ay, dad!

CAPTAIN. You've allowed your affections to drift into very shallow waters. Clap on all sail, and sheer off before you get aground.

POLLY. Ay, ay, dad! if wind and tide are with you. If not?

CAPTAIN. Drop an anchor to windward, and wait the turn of the tide.

POLLY. Ay, ay, dad! that suits me better. I think my little bark is sailing in deep water to a peaceful harbor; not drifting, dad, for I was taught by an old salt that the captain who allows his ship to drift is no sailor.

CAPTAIN. You're right there, Polly.

POLLY. But as you think there is danger, and it's too late to wear ship, over goes the anchor.

CAPTAIN. Too late! Are you in love with that monkey?

POLLY. I'm sure of it, dad.

CAPTAIN. Well, I'm not, and I forbid your having any thing more to do with him.

POLLY. Ay, ay, captain!

CAPTAIN. Captain! Why not dad, as usual?

POLLY. As you have taken command of my affections, I wish to pay proper respect to my superior officer.

CAPTAIN. Polly!

POLLY. Oh, it's all right, dad! You know better than I what's best for me; but he's so jolly and bright, and so kind-hearted, and — and — Oh, it's so hard to give him up! (*Sobs.*)

CAPTAIN. Who said any thing about giving him up? (*Takes her in his arms.*) O Polly, Polly, my pet, don't cry! You know I wouldn't stand in the way of your happiness. But such a boy!

POLLY. He's growing every day.

CAPTAIN. Yes, worse and worse. He can't splice a rope, nor reeve a block. Polly, I thought you were going to marry a sailor.

POLLY. Of my own making, yes. Teddy would sail with

us, and I could teach him; and when he is a real sailor we could marry. Don't you see, dad?

CAPTAIN. And are you willing to wait until that time?

POLLY. Forever, dad.

CAPTAIN. Then dry your eyes, pet; I consent. (*Aside.*) She'll die an old maid.

POLLY (*hugging him*). Oh, you dear old dad! May I run and tell him? (*Runs up* C.)

CAPTAIN. Belay, there! (POLLY *turns.*) Never disturb a sailor when he's on duty.

POLLY. Oh, he's no sailor! Eh, dad? Ha, ha, ha! (*Exit* C.)

CAPTAIN. Ah! she had me there, and she'll have him. Just like her mother; when she fell in love with me, I didn't know the compass from the caboose; but she waited, and so shall Master Ted. If there's the timber of a tar in him, I'll make him worthy of my Polly. (*Enter* MORGAN *from* R. 2; *slowly totters to chair,* R., *and sinks into it.*) Jack Ober at last. (*Turns his back to him.*)

MORGAN. Six days of misery, and no strength to rally! When the breeze brought the fragrance of that tropic paradise through my window, I felt its reviving freshness, and longed to be on deck; but on my feet my limbs refuse to do their duty, my head swims, and I totter like an old man in his dotage. What has brought me to this? not a week's illness? No, no! Remorse, the demon that has pursued me since that guilty night, is claiming its prey. There is no escape. (*Sees* CAPTAIN.) Ah! captain, you see I have weathered the storm. (*Attempts to rise: sinks back.*) Give me a helping hand.

CAPTAIN (*without turning*). I have no helping hand for Jack Ober.

MORGAN (*aghast*). Jack — Jack Ober! He knows me.

CAPTAIN. The man who swore eternal friendship with a messmate, then deserted him, left him to starve. The Judas who sold his honest heart for a money-belt! A thief! A helping-hand to such as you? No: I'd sooner cut it off, and cast it into the sea.

MORGAN. You are right, old messmate: I deserve your scorn. I did sell my honesty for gold, did desert you. Crush me, trample upon me; I deserve no man's help, no man's pity.

CAPTAIN (*turns*). O Jack, Jack! why did you do this thing, you who before that night deserved the title by which you were hailed, — honest Jack Ober?

MORGAN. Don't, Nat! don't call me that name.

CAPTAIN. And brave Jack Ober. Remember how you won that name. 'Twas when you saved the captain's child at Calcutta; and you deserved it.

MORGAN. Honest and brave. Titles to be defended by worthy actions and a pure life. When it came to the test, I, coward-like, deserted them. O Nat, I am an accursed wretch!

CAPTAIN. Belay, Jack! When you hand in the log of your voyage to the great underwriter up there, I'm afraid 'twill go hard with you : you've not sailed by compass. Let's leave that matter to Him. You say you're sorry, so, for the sake of the honest days, there's my hand.

MORGAN. No, no! I cannot take it: you don't know the worst of me. I — I — murdered Martin Secor.

CAPTAIN. Come, come, Jack, your head is still weak. Martin Secor was on deck an hour ago.

MORGAN. Yes, the impostor. The real Martin Secor followed me that night, swam after my boat, grappled it. I struck him down. (*Staggers to his feet.*) I see him now sinking, sinking, sinking; now he's gone, never to return. Will nothing blot out that horrid sight?

CAPTAIN. Jack, Jack, you rave! you are ill! let me call your daughter.

MORGAN. Ay! call her, call my son, to see their father on his knees, to hear him confess his crime, and implore pardon. (WOLF *rushes to* C. *from* L. 2.)

WOLF. Hush! The secrets of that night are ours alone. We three will settle them.

MORGAN. You here?

WOLF. To give you absolution if you repent.

MORGAN. Heaven knows I do.

WOLF. Then I am free to speak. When you struck at Martin Secor, you missed him, but he sank, encountering in his descent the trailing painter of your boat.

MORGAN. Ah!

WOLF. By this he sustained himself, and moved with you. Fearful that a second blow from your oar might prove fatal, he floated in silence until the boat was passing an island, when he abandoned it, and swam ashore. He was rescued in three days.

MORGAN. He still lives?

WOLF. He died ten years ago at Melbourne.

CAPTAIN. But who are you?

WOLF. His executor. There was a lad who, with one Nat Taylor, escaped to San Francisco. The faithful sailor fell ill. The lad, by a fortunate meeting, fell into the arms of his father. They sailed for Melbourne. On his deathbed the father told his story, and bade the boy seek the man who had wronged him, and wring a confession from him. These were his words : " Let not the friendship of man or the love of woman deter you from your purpose. He believes himself a murderer. His guilty soul will some time betray its secret; then, if but three words of repentance pass his lips, free him."

MORGAN. I am free at last, at last! (*Sinks weeping into chair*, R.)

CAPTAIN. But the boy, the little chap I took, where is he?

WOLF (*throws off wig and whiskers.* GRACE *appears* L. 1.) Here.

GRACE. Ah, Horace, Horace Gaylord! (*Runs into* WOLF'S *arms.*)

WOLF. Dear, dear Grace!

MORGAN. Horace Gaylord!

WOLF. To which add Secor, and you have my name.

GRACE. O Horace, what does this mean?

WOLF. That as my lady-love went off yachting without my permission, I had the curiosity to know why and where she was going.

GRACE. And you have been on board all the time, and never let me know you! and then the horrid names I called you! O Horace, what does it all mean?

WOLF. That three words have been spoken which make your father and me friends for life. (*Holds out hand to* MORGAN.)

MORGAN (*grasping it warmly*). For life. Grace, he's the prince of good fellows.

GRACE. A miracle! and he may marry your daughter?

MORGAN. To-morrow if he likes. I wish I had a dozen:

he should marry them all. (*Comes forward.*) Nat Taylor, old messmate, I'll take that hand now.

CAPTAIN.   Ay, ay, Jack, with the old Vulture grip! (*They shake hands warmly, and stand by* L. *table, conversing.* WOLF *and* GRACE *near* R. *table.* POLLY *and* TEDDY *appear* C., *hand in hand.*)

POLLY.   We've anchored, dad.

TEDDY.   She's swinging at her moorings (*swings* POLLY'S *hand*), and so am I. (*They come down* R.)

WOLF.   Don't forget to return my sou'wester, Ted.

TEDDY.   Hallo, Horace! have they found you out?

WOLF.   Yes: the stowaway is unmasked.

TEDDY.   Serves you right for bamboozling the whole company except me. The moment I cast my weather-eye on you, I saw through the disguise.

GRACE.   And you never told me!

POLLY.   Nor me. Smart, ain't you?

TEDDY.   Thank you, Polly. That's the first praise I have received for all my endeavors in the nautical line. The green hand's looking up.

(*Enter* CRUMBS R. I E. *with letter; keeps down extreme* R.)

CRUMBS (*to* TEDDY).   Look a-here, young ham-boner! dat ar' letter from de parson am written on one ob my bill ob fare. How de parson git dat? (*Enter* PHILLIS L. 2.)

TEDDY.   Ask the parson (*points to* PHILLIS) over there.

PHILLIS.   La, Mr. Crumbs! I stole it from the larder: I just fooled you to get rid of you.

CRUMBS.   O Phillis! how could you? O, dat ar' fill ob bear am de camel dat breaks de spell.

GRACE.   Now, Horace, tell me —

WOLF.   No more, Grace. Our troubles are over. Outward bound with favoring breezes, all looked bright before us. In mid-ocean we wrestled with the storm, but now all is fair and beautiful as we sail into port. Old messmates re-united —

MORGAN (*shaking hands with* CAPTAIN).   That's so, Nat.

CAPTAIN.   Ay, ay, Jack!

WOLF.   New loves budding —

TEDDY (*tucking* POLLY'S *arm into his*).   That means us, Polly: we are the buds.

WOLF.   True hearts united! (*Takes* GRACE *in his arms.*) Happiness complete! who can ask for more?

(CARTER *and* ARABELLA *appear* C. *on steps.*)

CARTER.   I can (*stretches out hand*).   "Divy."

ARABELLA (*throws her arms about his neck*).   My Grand Panjodah!

SLOW CURTAIN.

THE READING CLUB AND HANDY SPEAKER. Being selections in Prose and Poetry, Serious, Humorous, Pathetic, Patriotic, and Dramatic, for Readings and Recitations. Edited by GEORGE M. BAKER. Paper cover, fifteen cents each part.

CONTENTS OF READING-CLUB No. 1.

CONTENTS OF READING-CLUB No. 2.

CONTENTS OF READING-CLUB NO. 3.

CONTENTS OF READING-CLUB NO. 4.

CONTENTS OF READING-CLUB NO. 5.

CONTENTS OF READING-CLUB NO. 6.

CONTENTS OF READING-CLUB NO. 7.

CONTENTS OF READING-CLUB No 8.